CORK & FUZZ

Short and Tall

A Viking Easy-to-Read

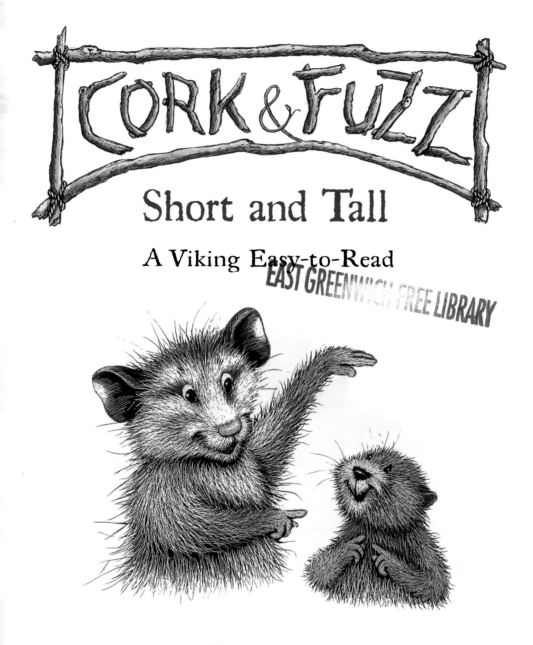

by **Dori Chaconas**

illustrated by **Lisa McCue**

VIKING

VIKING
Published by Penguin Group
Penguin Young Readers Group,
345 Hudson Street, New York, New York 10014, U.S.A.
Penguin Group (Canada), 90 Eglinton Avenue East, Suite 700, Toronto,
Ontario, Canada M4P 2Y3 (a division of Pearson Penguin Canada Inc.)
Penguin Books Ltd, 80 Strand, London WC2R 0RL, England
Penguin Ireland, 25 St Stephen's Green, Dublin 2, Ireland (a division of Penguin Books Ltd)
Penguin Group (Australia), 250 Camberwell Road, Camberwell, Victoria 3124, Australia
(a division of Pearson Australia Group Pty Ltd)
Penguin Books India Pvt Ltd, 11 Community Centre, Panchsheel Park,
New Delhi - 110 017, India
Penguin Group (NZ), Cnr Airborne and Rosedale Roads, Albany,
Auckland 1310, New Zealand (a division of Pearson New Zealand Ltd)
Penguin Books (South Africa) (Pty) Ltd, 24 Sturdee Avenue, Rosebank,
Johannesburg 2196, South Africa

Penguin Books Ltd, Registered Offices: 80 Strand, London WC2R 0RL, England

Published in 2006 by Viking, a division of Penguin Young Readers Group

1 3 5 7 9 10 8 6 4 2

LIBRARY OF CONGRESS CATALOGING-IN-PUBLICATION DATA
Chaconas, Dori, date-
Cork and Fuzz : short and tall / by Dori Chaconas ; illustrated by Lisa McCue.
p. cm.
Summary: The friendship between Cork, a muskrat, and Fuzz, a possum,
is in trouble when Cork decides that since he is older, he has to be taller than Fuzz.
ISBN 0-670-05985-4 (hardcover)
[1. Size—Fiction. 2. Opossums—Fiction. 3. Muskrat—Fiction. 4. Best friends—Fiction. 5.
Friendship—Fiction.] I. Title: Short and tall. II. McCue, Lisa, ill. III. Title.
PZ7.C342Cor 2006
[E]—dc22
2004017393

Viking® and Easy-to-Read® are registered trademarks of Penguin Group (USA) Inc.

Manufactured in China
Set in Bookman
Book design by Kelley McIntyre

Reading level: 1.7

For Steven James, my star
—D. C.

To Max, who'll be
learning to read soon
—L. M.

Chapter One

Cork was a short muskrat.

He ate cattails and roots.

Fuzz was a tall possum.

He ate berries and seeds,

pancakes,

hamburger buns,

apple peels,

candy wrappers,

worms,

and black beetles.

One short muskrat.

One tall possum.

Two best friends.

One day, Cork looked up at Fuzz's head.

"Something is not right," Cork said.

"What is not right?" Fuzz asked.

"I am older than you," Cork said.

"But you are taller than me."

"Are you standing in a hole?" Fuzz asked.

Cork looked down.

"I am not standing in a hole. You are

taller than me."

"Does it matter that I am taller than you?"

Fuzz asked.

"I am older," Cork said. "I need to be

taller. It is a rule."

"I am sorry," Fuzz said. "I did not mean

to break a rule."

"Do you think you can be shorter?"

Cork asked.

Fuzz's tail dropped into the dirt.

"I do not know how to be shorter,"

he said.

"Think, think, think," Cork said.

"We will think about how to make

you shorter."

"Lunch, lunch, lunch," Fuzz said.

"I will think about eating lunch."

He picked up a beetle.

He opened his mouth wide.

"Do not eat that beetle!"

Cork yelled.

He grabbed Fuzz's snout.

"If you stop eating, you will stop growing! Then you will not be taller than me."

"*Umma-umma-umma!*" Fuzz tried to speak.

Cork let go of Fuzz's snout.

"*Stop eating?*" Fuzz shouted. "*Me?*"

"Just for a little while," Cork said.

"How long is a little while?" Fuzz looked worried.

"Not long," Cork said. "About . . . seven days."

Fuzz groaned.

Chapter Two

"While we are waiting for you to not grow," Cork said, "can you walk on your knees? That will make you shorter."

Fuzz groaned again.

Cork walked along the path on his feet.

Fuzz walked along the path on his knees.

"Ouch!" Fuzz said.

"What is the matter?" Cork asked.

"My knee stepped on a stick," Fuzz said.

They took three more steps.

Fuzz yelled again. "Ouch! Ouch!"

"What is the matter now?" Cork asked.

"My knee stepped on a nut."

They took three more steps. Fuzz yelled
again. "Ouch! Ouch! *Ouch!*"

"What did your knee step on now?"
Cork asked.

"This time it is not my knee that hurts,"
Fuzz said. "This time it is my stomach
that hurts. Because it is empty!"

Cork sighed. "This is not going to work."

"I cannot be shorter," Fuzz said. "But
maybe we can make you taller."

"Oh, yes," said Cork. "We can make
me taller!"

"Possums eat good food!" Fuzz said.
"Maybe you need to eat like a possum.
Then you will grow like a possum."

"What did you eat for breakfast?" Cork asked.

"I ate three beetles. I ate four worms. I ate two pancakes."

"I hope there are some pancakes left," Cork said.

"Nope," said Fuzz. "But here is a nice fat worm!"

"Uck," said Cork. "Do I have to eat it?"

"Do you want to grow?" Fuzz asked.

"Yes," said Cork. He closed his eyes. He opened his mouth.

Chapter Three

"I cannot eat this worm!" Cork said.

"Maybe possums do something else to

make them tall."

Fuzz popped the worm into his own mouth.

"We hang from tree branches," he said.

Cork jumped up and down.

"I can hang from a branch!" he said.

"I can stretch!"

"We hang by our tails," Fuzz said.

Cork looked at his short tail.

"My tail cannot do that."

"You can hang by your paws!" Fuzz said.

Cork jumped up and down again.

"Yes!" he said. "I can hang by my paws!"

Cork stood on Fuzz's back.

He grabbed a branch in the nut tree.

Fuzz moved away.

Cork's feet swung in the air.

"Do I have to hang here long?" Cork asked.

"Not long," Fuzz said. "About . . .

seven days."

Cork wiggled. "I have a problem."

"What kind of problem?" Fuzz asked.

"A seed puff blew up my nose," Cork said.

"Now I have an itch."

"Scratch it," said Fuzz.

"If I scratch it, I will fall," Cork said.

"Can you wait?" Fuzz asked.

"No," Cork said. "I cannot wait.

It is a bad itch."

"Can you sneeze it out?" Fuzz asked.

"Ka-*chee*!" Cork sneezed. "Ka-*chee*!"

"I cannot sneeze it out!"

"I will help," Fuzz said.

He picked up a long stick.

Chapter Four

"What are you doing with that
stick?" Cork asked.

"I will scratch the itch for you," Fuzz said.

"You will poke me in the eye!" Cork said.

"I will be careful," Fuzz said.

The stick did not poke Cork in the eye.

It poked Cork in the belly.

"Ouch!" Cork yelled.

Then he fell on Fuzz.

"Ooof!" The seed puff blew out of
Cork's nose.

"Ooof!" The air blew out of Fuzz's belly.

"I am sorry I fell on you," Cork said.

"I am sorry you have not gotten taller,"
Fuzz said. "Or lighter."

Cork helped Fuzz to his feet. Then he

shook Fuzz's paw.

"It was nice being best friends," Cork said.

"But we *are* best friends!" Fuzz said.

"No," said Cork. "We are too different.

I am older than you. You are taller

than me. There is no way to change that.

Good-bye, Fuzz."

Cork walked toward his home in the pond.

Fuzz looked after him. He sniffed.

"Good-bye, Cork," he whispered.

A tear slipped out of his eye

and landed on a nut.

Fuzz picked up the nut.

Then he picked up another nut.

He jumped up

and ran after Cork.

"Cork!" he yelled. "Wait!"

When Fuzz reached Cork, he
held out the two nuts.

"See these nuts?" Fuzz said.

"Are they the same?"

"No," Cork said. "One is big
and wet. One is little and dry."

"They are different," Fuzz said.

"But they are still nuts."

Then Fuzz pulled Cork

to the edge of the pond.

They looked at themselves in the water.

"See these friends?" Fuzz asked.

"Are they the same?"

"No," Cork said. "One is short. One is tall."

"They are different," Fuzz said.

"But they are still friends."

"Just like two nuts?" Cork asked.

"One little and one big?"